# JOEY

### JACK KENT

**Prentice-Hall Books for Young Readers**
A Division of Simon & Schuster, Inc., New York

CHAPTER II FUNDS

Published by Prentice-Hall Books for Young Readers
A Division of Simon & Schuster, Inc.
Simon & Schuster Building
Rockefeller Center
1230 Avenue of the Americas
New York, NY 10020

10 9 8 7 6 5 4 3

10 9 8 7 6 5 4 3 2 1 pbk

Prentice-Hall Books for Young Readers
is a trademark of Simon & Schuster, Inc.
Manufactured in the United States of America

Library of Congress Cataloging in Publication Data
Kent, Jack, 1920-
Joey.
Summary: Joey, a young kangaroo, becomes bored playing alone
in his mother's pouch and invites some friends over to play with him.
[1. Kangaroos—Fiction.   2. Play—Fiction] I. Title.
PZ7.K414Jo 1984      [E]      84-4694
ISBN 0-13-510348-7
ISBN 0-13-510355-X pbk

To Naomi and Michael

Once there was a little kangaroo named Joey.
His mother worried about him, as mothers do.
She worried that Joey might get lost.

So, to keep track of him,
she put Joey in her pocket.

It was comfortable in mother's pocket. Joey had his coloring books and his toys to play with there. But he was lonely for someone his own age.

"I want to go play with my friends," said Joey.
"Ask your friends to come HERE and play," said mother.

So Joey invited his friend Billy.

And he invited his friend Betty.

And he invited his friend Bob.
And they all came to visit.

At first Joey's friends had fun bouncing around in mother's pocket.

But after a while they wanted to do something else.
"Let's watch TV," said Billy.

"I don't have a TV," said Joey.
"I'll get mine," Billy said.

And he did.

At first they couldn't
get a good picture.

"Is that better?" asked Billy.
"Much better," said Bob.
"But there aren't any programs
worth watching," said Betty.

"Let's play some records."
"I don't have a record player,"
said Joey.
"I'll get my stereo," said Bob.

And he did.
Betty and Billy helped.

They listened to the music and danced.

"We've played all the records,"
said Billy. "Now what?"

"Let's form a band and play
our OWN music," said Betty.
"I have a guitar," said Joey.

Billy and Betty and Bob
ran to get their instruments.

Bob brought his horn.

Billy brought his drums.

And Betty brought her piano.

# "THAT WILL DO!"

said mother.

"OUT! OUT! Everybody out!" she said
Out went the TV and the stereo. Out went Bob and his horn.

Out went Billy and his drums.

Out went Betty and her piano.

And out went Joey.

**"OOPS!"**

said mother.
"I didn't mean to
throw YOU out!"

"Well, as long as I AM out,"
said Joey, "may I go play?"

"Yes," Mother said with a deep sigh.
"But don't get lost."